9/12/17

W9-AQI-483

GOODBYE SUMMER, HELLO AUTUMN

KENARD PAK

Henry Holt and Company New York

Hello, late summer morning.

Hello, trees.

Hello! Now that the cool winds have come,
we love how our branches sway in the sun.

Hello, playful foxes and singing blue jays.

Hello! We are busy looking for food.
Some of us are heading south to our winter homes.

Hello, walking stick and butterflies.

Hello! We're surprised you saw us. We try our best to blend in, and we'll do the same in warmer places.

Hello, beavers.
Hello, chipmunks.

Hello! We have no time to play because we're making cozy nests and dens. It will be cold soon, and we want to get ready.

Hello, flowers.

Hello! We are leaning into the sun, enjoying the last summer rays. Some of us, like asters and phlox, are late bloomers. We make the end of the season even more colorful.

Hello, thunder.

Hello! You can hear my low rumble from far away.
My clouds loom over the open fields and quiet hills.

Hello, breezy wind.

Hello! I love to *whoosh* drizzle and leaves through the misty streets.

Hello! It's time to bring out your thick sweaters and scarves.

Hello! Now that the wind has come, I often get covered with fallen leaves.

Hello, leaves.

Hello! We are changing our colors. Some of us turn red or brown, while others turn gold or yellow. The dogwood leaves turn purple!

Hello, big orange sun.

Hello! I am setting earlier and earlier now that summer is coming to an end, but I will see you again tomorrow.

Goodbye, summer. . . .

Hello, autumn!

For Ed and Minh

Henry Holt and Company, LLC
Publishers since 1866
175 Fifth Avenue
New York, New York 10010
mackids.com

Henry Holt® is a registered trademark of Henry Holt and Company, LLC.
Copyright © 2016 by Kenard Pak
All rights reserved.

Library of Congress Cataloging-in-Publication Data
Goodbye summer, hello autumn / Kenard Pak.—First edition.
Pak, Kenard, author, illustrator.
pages   cm
Summary: "In a simple, evocative conversation with nature, a young girl witnesses how the season
changes from summer to autumn"—Provided by publisher.
ISBN 978-1-62779-415-2 (hardback)
[1. Nature—Fiction. 2. Seasons—Fiction. 3. Summer—Fiction. 4. Autumn—Fiction.] I. Title.
PZ7.1.P354Go 2016   [E]—dc23   2015014262

Our books may be purchased in bulk for promotional, educational, or business use. Please contact your local bookseller or the
Macmillan Corporate and Premium Sales Department at (800) 221-7945 ext. 5442 or by e-mail at MacmillanSpecialMarkets@macmillan.com.

First Edition—2016 / Designed by Kenard Pak and April Ward
The artist used watercolor and pencil, digitally enhanced, to create the illustrations for this book.
Printed in China by RR Donnelley Asia Printing Solutions Ltd., Dongguan City, Guangdong Province
3   5   7   9   10   8   6   4